God's Kiss©

Mrs. Seebo's Classic Fables™

Author/Donna Seebo • Illustrator/Ed Gedrose

God's Kiss

Published By:

Mrs. Seebo's Classic Fables™

PO Box 97272 • Tacoma, Washington • 98497
206-582-5604 • 1-800-872-8852 • Fax: 206-582-5597

Illustrator/Ed Gedrose

Edited By/ Susie Miller

Project Coordinator/Graphic Design:
Peter J. Slaney • Creative Director
PO Box 231 Troutdale, Oregon 97060
503-669-0353

ISBN# 1-883164-01-X

Color Separation and Printing in Hong Kong through Amica International of Seattle.

*This Book Is Dedicated To Children
Of All Ages Throughout The World.*

*"Dreams Are Windows
Into Another World."*

A small white country chapel with a tall wooden steeple is filled with the sounds of Christmas music. It stands with dignity, covered with freshly fallen snow. The strains of "Silent Night" float from the little church. It is Christmas eve and snow is beginning to fall once again. The effects are magical.

In the darkness, the last chords of "Silent Night" fade softly, their echoes muffled by the falling snow. The little church stands quietly, the soft glow of its lights spilling a message of peace and warmth through its stained-glass windows.

"Johnny, Johnny, wake up! It's late!"

A hand gently shakes the shoulder of a little boy who, during the church service, has fallen sound asleep. Johnny awakens reluctantly. He has had a special dream and he doesn't want to leave its happiness and serenity but he has no choice.

Getting up slowly out of the church pew he sleepily stands still while his mother bundles him up in a cherry red jacket and hood to protect him against the cold outside.

"Come on Johnny, let's go home," says his mother.

Placing his hand in his mother's, Johnny walks out to the car, stumbling now and then, as he is still half asleep. When they arrive at their car, Johnny leans against his mother's leg hardly able to keep his eyes open.

He feels strong arms surround him and lift him up, placing him on the back seat.

"Little tyke sure was good tonight, Mrs. Leslie. It's usually pretty hard for a little'un like that to make it through an evening without fussing!"

"Yes, he was unusually good, Adam. Thanks for putting him in the car for me."

"Sure, anytime! He's no small pack of potatoes that boy. Have a nice Christmas!"

"Merry Christmas, Adam. Good night!" Mrs. Leslie gets into her car and starts the long drive home through the snow. It will be at least an hour before they'll be there. "A white Christmas! Johnny will be so pleased!"

She smiles happily to herself as she thinks of the new sled she has gotten for Johnny, knowing how thrilled he will be trying it out on Christmas morning.

Johnny, meanwhile, curled up and sleeping on the back seat, is totally unaware of all that has gone on about him. He has reentered his dream world and is now living an adventure which he will always call "GOD'S CHRISTMAS KISS".

Johnny finds himself at the entrance to a large, open valley, framed by high mountains rich in the brown red colors of the earth. He stands in awe, even a little fearful, of the mountain's great size. After all, he is just a little boy and not very tall.

Well, why are you standing there Johnny?. Go into the valley! Johnny is startled. He can't imagine who spoke, there is no one around.

"Caw! Caw! Time's a-wasting! Move along! Move along!" Looking about, Johnny notices a super sized crow nervously flapping its wings. "Did you just speak to me?" asks the amazed Johnny.

"Of course, I did! What do you think I am, a mute? children!"

The Crow sounds very disgusted.

"Gee, I'm sorry. I didn't mean to hurt your feelings. Just never had a crow talk to me before!," says Johnny quietly.

"Of course you have!" says the Crow. "You just never listened! Oh, no matter, you must hurry enter the valley of the animals, for tonight there is to be a special gathering and you are one of the last to arrive. Hurry! Hurry! Follow me!"

With these words, the crow
begins to flap his wings
vigorously, rising high into the
air, then dips down just in front
of Johnny.

"Follow me! he caws. "Follow me!"

Johnny follows as he is told. It is
all he can do to keep up with the fast
flying crow. He falls once but hardly
pays attention. He isn't concerned over
anything but reaching that special destination.

While Johnny is so intent on following crow, he fails to
notice the family of grey bunnies that watch his actions from
their burrow beneath a tall green pine.

"Goodness, there's always one that's late. We'd best be
getting along too!" Gently prodding her six babies
with her pink nose, Mama Bunny proceeds to
lead her family to the destination, taking
their own special shortcut to be there
in prime time.

Johnny feels like he has been following Crow for such a long time when suddenly he hears, "Take your place! Take your place in the circle!" Stopping in amazement Johnny looks upon a scene he never could have imagined. He sees a large open area of valley ground, covered with a thick green grass. In the open space are many other children and animals. All kinds of animals. And all of the animals are talking! He can understand every word they are saying.

Noticing Johnny's arrival, the animals and children greet him.

"Hi Johnny! We've been waiting for you. Here, come take your place in the circle." Everyone is filled with such joy and happiness. A unique feeling of expectancy fills the air and Johnny's curiosity is aroused.

Close to Johnny is a little Skunk, who is talking excitedly to a green and black snake coiled up next to him. "This is my first time. Have you felt God's Kiss before?" little Skunk asks the gentle Snake.

"Oh, yes!" says gentle Snake, "But each time it is so special you can never describe it. You just have to feel it!"

"Oh, I can hardly wait!" says little Skunk.

"Excuse me, but what is God's Kiss?" asks Johnny. "And why is this night so special? Why do all the animals talk? I don't understand." Questions come tumbling one after another from Johnny's mouth.

The gentle Snake looks at the little Skunk and says, "He's a new one. We should explain." Gentle Snake slides over to Johnny.

"I will tell you. This is the "Sacred Valley of Life", where only children of kind and gentle thoughts can come in their dreams, and where we animals can live in harmony and peace. Each year at a special time a call is sent out to all of us to gather here. Children, special ones, are allowed to share our Valley on this very sacred night and know the gift and blessing of God's Kiss. You as a child may come only once but we animals come each year. It is a special occasion to be remembered all of your life."

"But what is God's Kiss?" asks Johnny.

"You'll soon see for yourself—it's almost time." Crawling quickly back to his place in the circle, gentle Snake coils himself into a comfortable position, patiently waiting.

"SILENCE!!!!" a voice thunders. Following the sound's direction, Johnny realizes that a large golden cat has given the order.

Everything and everyone becomes still as still can be. Johnny notices the beauty of the valley and the wondrous array of animals he has never seen before.

The atmosphere is so peaceful...when ever so gently and quietly a golden light begins to fill the valley. It becomes stronger and stronger in intensity and color. It covers and illuminates individually every form of life that has gathered here in the valley. Johnny feels its warmth of love and peace surround him in a way only he could know and understand. The light pulsates and Johnny is wishing he could stay within its form forever.

Then, the light starts to slowly withdraw itself from all in the valley until the sky above can be clearly seen. The sky is bright with thousands of stars that sparkle in neon colors—reds, blues, greens and yellows.

Not one word is whispered but anticipation fills each who waits.

Small white flakes begin to fall. One falls on little Skunk's nose. "I've been given God's Kiss!" he exclaims.

Everyone lifts their faces to receive God's Kiss. Johnny whispers to himself as two snowflakes fall on his face, one on each cheek, "I've been kissed twice! God has kissed me twice!" He watches the other children and animals. He sees all of them given God's Kiss. The earth, trees and all forms of life are "Kissed", not one forgotten.

Johnny's mother finally arrives home. The snow is coming down quite heavily now as she drives the car into the driveway. Her husband, seeing her arrive, quickly goes out to the car to help carry Johnny inside. Opening the car door, he reaches for Johnny, picks him up and lifts him out.

"Honey, this boy is in a deep sleep."

"Yes, I know, dear. He is so very tired."

Johnny sleepily stirs in his fathers arms saying, "God kissed me, Daddy!"

"Of course he did son," says his father. "Of course he did." Smiling to himself, he takes the sleeping child into the house.

While tucking his son into bed, Johnny's father
turns to his wife and says' "I don't know what Johnny
is dreaming, but I sure wish I could share it with him!"

Published By:

Mrs. Seebo's Classic Fables™

To order additional books or talking book tapes
call:**1-800-40-FABLE** or fax: **1-206-582-5597**

For information on other upcoming publications
or if you have any comments please write to.

Mrs. Seebo's Classic Fables™
PO Box 97272 • Tacoma, Washington • 98497
206-582-5604

Other publications by Mrs. Seebo's Classic Fables™

Mind Magic©, Audio Cassette Package